FOCUS ON THE FAMILY PRESENTS

THE IMAGINATION STATION

Freedom at the Falls

BOOK 22

MARIANNE HERING AND SHEILA SEIFERT
ILLUSTRATIONS BY SERGIO CARIELLO

TYNDALE

FOCUS ON THE FAMILY • ADVENTURES IN ODYSSEY®
TYNDALE HOUSE PUBLISHERS, INC. • CAROL STREAM, ILLINOIS

In memory of Elbert Sloan,
who never learned to read

Freedom at the Falls

© 2018 Focus on the Family. All rights reserved.

A Focus on the Family book published by Tyndale House Publishers, Inc., Carol Stream, Illinois 60188.

The Imagination Station, Adventures in Odyssey, and *Focus on the Family* and their accompanying logos and designs are federally registered trademarks of Focus on the Family, 8605 Explorer Drive, Colorado Springs, CO 80920.

TYNDALE and Tyndale's quill logo are registered trademarks of Tyndale House Publishers, Inc.

Cover design by Michael Heath | Magnus Creative

For Library of Congress Cataloging-in-Publication Data for this title, visit http://www.loc.gov/help/contact-general.html.

For manufacturing information regarding this product, please call 1-800-323-9400.

For information about special discounts for bulk purchases, please contact Tyndale House Publishers at csresponse@tyndale.com, or call 1-800-323-9400.

Printed in the United States of America

ISBN: 9-781-58997-979-6

24   23   22   21   20   19
7   6   5   4   3   2

Contents

The Imagination Station

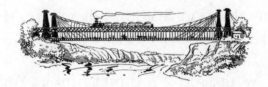

Patrick and Beth hurried down the stairs at Whit's End. Beth's galoshes squeaked on each step. The cousins entered the workshop where Whit created his inventions.

Tables and boxes filled the room. Computer parts and small engine motors lay on the tables. Stacks of recycling materials leaned against the walls.

The Imagination Station was one of Whit's

inventions. It stood in the corner. This one had been made from a Model T car.

Whit was standing behind a long, wood workbench. "Hello," he said. "Are you ready for a President's Day adventure?"

"I remember meeting George Washington in an Imagination Station adventure," Patrick said.

"Yes," Whit said. "You met him at Yorktown in 1781. It was at the end of the American Revolution."

"That adventure was scary and fun at the same time," Beth said. "I've always wanted to meet Abraham Lincoln. I'd like to feel his whiskers."

Whit laughed and said, "A little girl about your age asked Mr. Lincoln to grow a beard. It was just before he took office as president in 1861."

Whit stroked his own chin and then said, "That gives me an idea."

"Are you going to grow a beard?" Patrick asked.

Whit shook his head. He said, "How would you like to help Honest Abe with a little problem?"

"Yes!" the cousins shouted.

"What are we going to bring him?" Patrick asked. "A tall black hat?"

"No," Whit said. "Mr. Lincoln already has a stovepipe hat." He reached under the table and pulled out a black bag. The fabric was shiny and slick.

Whit handed the bag to Patrick.

Patrick lifted it. "It's not heavy," Patrick said.

"And it's not fragile," Whit said. "But don't lose it. Mr. Lincoln will want it."

Beth saw a smile tug at Whit's lips. The inventor's eyes twinkled mysteriously.

"Are we ready?" Beth asked.

"Not yet," Whit said. "I also have something for Mary."

"Who's Mary?" Beth asked.

Whit said, "Mary Todd Lincoln is the First Lady, Mrs. Lincoln." He pulled a disk of polished wood out of his apron pocket.

Whit held it up for Beth to see.

The disk was a little larger than a quarter. It was cut from a cross section of a branch. Beth could see the tree rings and the bark around the edges. The disk had a bird design on it. There was a small hole at the top. A thin white ribbon was threaded through the hole to make it a necklace.

Whit said, "Keep the necklace hidden until you see its twin."

"I don't understand," Beth said. "Isn't this for Mary?"

"You'll know the answer to that in good time," Whit said.

Beth heard a noise. She turned toward the sound. She saw Patrick sitting inside the Imagination Station. He was in the driver's seat, the bag on his lap.

Beth hurried to the Model T. She sat in the passenger's seat. A white bird feather was on the seat. *This is left over from the last adventure*, Beth thought.

"Where's Eugene?" Beth asked. "Did he ever come back from his tour with Mr. Tesla?"

Whit nodded and said, "He's fixing the time glitch with Mr. Tesla's help. He isn't happy being nearly eighty years old."

Whit waved goodbye. Beth and Patrick waved back.

Patrick took hold of the steering wheel. He turned the wheel with a jerk.

The car seemed to surge forward in the workshop. But everything Beth saw through the windshield blurred. She saw only a million dots of color spinning.

Then the dots broke apart. They sprayed out of the machine like water droplets.

We're driving through time, Beth thought.

And then suddenly, everything went black.

The Slave Catcher

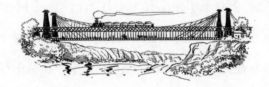

Patrick opened his eyes. He and Beth were standing on a wooden platform. In one hand he held a train ticket.

A grown-up bumped against him. Others pushed to get on a train. A noisy crowd surrounded them.

"There are American flags all over the train," Beth said. The steam locomotive's smokestack looked like a parade float. A brass band was playing "The Star-Spangled

Banner." The platform was too crowded for Patrick and Beth to see the band.

The Imagination Station faded and then disappeared.

Patrick looked down. The black bag was at his feet. He poked it with his toe. He was wearing shoes with tiny black buttons on the side. He was also wearing a gray wool cloak. Under it was a loose-fitting, light-brown suit.

He looked at Beth. She wore a fancy green dress with white trim. The petticoats made the dress billow out like a parachute. A green velvet cloak hung over her shoulders. The cloak's hood covered her head.

The early morning sun shone brightly, but it was still windy and cold.

"Patrick," Beth said, "I have two train tickets for Saturday, February 16, 1861. The trip goes from Cleveland, Ohio, to Buffalo, New York."

"Two tickets?" Patrick said. "Then we have an extra one." He held up his own ticket.

Beth said, "Maybe the extra ticket is a mistake."

Patrick looked at the ticket. "You're right," he said. "This one is for the Black Rock Ferry into Canada." He shrugged and stuffed the ticket into his pants pocket.

A discarded page of newspaper blew in his direction. It wrapped around his shin. Patrick pulled it off. He read the headline out loud: "'Supporters in Buffalo Await Lincoln's Arrival.'"

"What else does it say?" Beth asked.

Patrick skimmed the article. "This is Mr. Lincoln's inaugural train," he said. He looked at Beth. "Does *inaugural* mean the beginning of Mr. Lincoln's presidency?"

"I'm pretty sure that's it," she said. "Presidents have to give an inaugural speech when they take office."

Patrick read more of the article. "He's been on the train about a week so far," he said. "He has another week of stops. Then he gives the speech on March fourth."

"Then I say we board this train!" Beth said. "Maybe we'll get to meet Mr. Lincoln." She handed one of the tickets to Patrick.

Other people pressed around them. The passengers were mostly men. They looked important in their dark suits and brimmed hats.

A pile of luggage was heaped in front of a car that was right behind the coal car. It had a wide, sliding door. One railroad crewmember was loading bags into the car.

"That's the baggage car," Beth said. "Let's board one of the passenger cars."

A hiss of steam left the locomotive's smokestack.

"The engine is starting!" Patrick said. He

picked up the bag and hurried toward the train.

Beth lifted her skirt a few inches and hurried after him.

The cousins headed toward a narrow door at the end of the second passenger car. They climbed three metal steps to a small platform outside the door. They each offered their ticket to a man in a black cap.

The man said, "You're just in time. Welcome to the Lincoln Special. I'm Conductor Nottingham." He took the tickets from each cousin's hand. He used a ticket punch to mark them. Then he handed the tickets back.

Patrick put his ticket in his pocket. Beth slipped hers into her cloak pocket. The cousins stepped inside the train.

Nottingham shouted, "All aboard!" and shut the door.

Patrick looked for a place to sit. But

businessmen filled every velvet-covered bench. They were talking and laughing together. Servants had to stand and were gathered at the back of the car.

A small wood-burning stove was in the center of the car. It gave out heat and a little smoke.

"Where do we go?" Patrick asked. He set Lincoln's bag on the floor near the stove.

"Let's ask the conductor where Mr. Lincoln is," Beth said.

Patrick scanned the passenger car. Nottingham was talking to the servants at the back.

Across the aisle, a rugged-looking man leaned against one wall. The man had blond hair. He wore a long leather coat with a star-shaped badge. The fabric of his pants was thick. His brown boots went nearly to his knees.

"Maybe the man with the badge knows," Patrick said, pointing to him. The cousins moved toward the man.

The man saw them coming. He opened his jacket and reached inside a pocket.

Patrick glimpsed a revolver in a holster on the man's hip. A coiled whip also hung from his belt. Patrick wondered if the man was a sheriff.

The man pulled out a folded poster. He opened it so Patrick and Beth could see it.

WANTED

Isobel Culver, also known as "Sally"

Reward $450

for information leading to her capture.

Light brown skin. Intelligent expression.

Brand on her left shoulder.

The scared face of a teen slave stared at them. Patrick read the words above the picture: "Wanted, Isobel Culver, also known as 'Sally.'"

Below the picture were these words: "Reward: $450 for information leading to her capture."

Patrick was stunned. He read the man's badge. It said, "Runaway Slave Patrol."

The man said, "Sally escaped from a good home in Lexington, Kentucky. I got a tip that she's on this train. I'll give you part of the reward—fifty silver pieces—if you help me find her."

Patrick shook his head. "No," he said, "not for a million dollars."

Beth's stomach flip-flopped. She felt ill. She had never dreamed she would meet a slave catcher.

"My name is Holman Jones," the man said. "What are you staring at, miss?"

Beth felt confused. "I'm sorry for being rude," she said. "But aren't we in the North, where slavery is illegal?"

"That's right. We're in Ohio," Jones said.

"Then go back to the South," Patrick said. "No one can own a slave in Ohio."

The man chuckled. "This badge doesn't mean I can *own* a slave in Ohio," he said. "It means I can *capture* runaway slaves—legally. Then I return them to their owners."

"For money," Patrick said.

"That's right, young man," Jones said. "I get paid for lawful, hard work. Slaves are property. If someone stole your horse, you'd want it back, wouldn't you?"

Beth crossed her arms and glared at Jones. "A person is not an animal," she said.

Jones laughed. "Of course not," he said. "A good slave is worth more money than a horse!" His eyes narrowed. "For instance, what if *you* were a runaway slave?" He poked Beth in the shoulder with his finger. "I could take you back to your master and get a reward."

15

"You couldn't do that!" Patrick said. "She's not a slave."

A sinister smile formed on the slave catcher's lips. "Who's to say?" Jones asked. He looked Beth over. "You could be of mixed race. Your hair is as black as a Negro's."

He reached over and fingered a lock of Beth's dark hair.

Beth slapped his hand away. Her face flushed red with fury. "And what if I am of mixed race?" she said. "God loves everybody the same. And that's what counts."

"You sound religious," Jones said. "Like a Quaker."

Beth knew Quakers were Christians. She guessed they were against slavery from what Jones said. She said, "I'm glad to sound like a Christian. *You* sound like the devil, full of lies."

Jones sneered at Beth. He briskly walked

over to a group of men. He showed them the poster.

Beth's temper was still fired up. She closed her eyes and took a deep breath. At the same time, she felt Patrick nudge her.

Beth turned toward him. "I don't care if using that word is bad manners," she said. "He does sound like the devil."

"It's not that," Patrick said. He looked ill.

"Then what?" Beth asked, confused.

"Mr. Lincoln's bag," Patrick said. "I lost it."

Sally

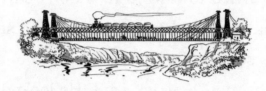

Beth took Patrick's hand. "We'll go back to the last place you had it," she said. Beth led him toward the stove. She said, "Show me where you put the bag."

Patrick tapped a spot with his shoe.

"Are you sure?" Beth asked.

"Yes," Patrick said. "Maybe Mr. Nottingham picked it up."

"We can ask," Beth said. "He's done talking now." They went to him.

The conductor said, "All personal items are stored in the baggage car. It's toward the front of the train. It's still unlocked. You'll have to go through the smoking car first." He bowed to Beth, nodded to Patrick, and left.

The cousins crossed over a connection platform. Patrick pushed open the door of the next passenger car. A cloud of smoke billowed out. He fanned away some of the smoke with his hand. Then he stepped inside.

The seats were full in this car too. As many as a dozen men stood, holding on to railings or bench backs. The entire car smelled of cigar smoke.

Patrick saw several men he thought were reporters. They were sitting and scribbling in notebooks.

The cousins passed through the car. They crossed over the platform connecting the smoking car to the baggage car.

Patrick looked around inside the baggage car. On one wall was a large sliding door. On the opposite was a stack of trunks, wooden crates, and carpetbags. Above it was a row of windows.

He picked up the nearest black bag.

"Wait," Beth said, "how do you know that's the right one?"

 Patrick looked around the baggage car again. One other black bag was perched near the top of the heap.

"This one feels like the right weight," Patrick said. "But I'd better check that one just to make sure."

Patrick stepped on a trunk to reach the bag. He lifted it, but the bag was too heavy. He dropped it, and the luggage stack moved. A flowered carpetbag tumbled down and revealed a small hideaway. Patrick couldn't believe what he saw.

"Sally?" he said.

Beth stepped on top of a crate so she could see the runaway.

The teen climbed out of the hideaway space. Beth thought she was much prettier in person than on the poster.

Sally was wearing a plain, long brown dress. It had a high neck and long sleeves. Her skin was a beautiful light brown. A few freckles dusted her cheeks.

WANTED

Isobel Culver, also known as "Sally"

Reward $450

for information leading to her capture.

Light brown skin. Intelligent expression.

Brand on her left shoulder.

"You must have met Holman Jones if you know my name," she said in a soft voice.

Patrick stepped off the trunk. "Jones is on the train," he said. "He's showing the poster with your face on it to all the passengers.

He's offering money to anyone who helps find you."

Sally seemed to shrink at the news. "Are you going to tell him where I am?" she asked.

"No!" Beth said, stepping off the box. "Don't worry. We won't turn you in. We'll even help if we can." Beth introduced herself and Patrick.

Then Beth noticed that Sally was wearing a necklace. It was identical to the one Whit had given to her. The twin. She gasped.

Beth pulled out her own necklace from underneath her dress.

Sally smiled sweetly, showing straight white teeth. She said, "Which one of you is the conductor?"

Beth didn't know what she was talking about.

And it seemed Patrick didn't either. "Conductor?" Patrick said. "I don't work for the railroad."

Sally's forehead creased in a slight frown. "Aren't you with the Underground Railroad?" she asked. "That necklace is a secret signal."

Beth had more questions. But Patrick said, "We shouldn't be talking. Someone might hear us. And I have to take this bag to Mr. Lincoln."

A loud whistle blew, and the train began to slow.

"Mr. Lincoln gives a short speech at almost every stop," Sally said. "When the train stops, go out the side door to the back. Mr. Lincoln will be on the rear platform, greeting people."

"Good," Beth said. "I don't want to pass Mr. Jones again."

Sally put her hand on Beth's arm. "Whatever you do," she said, "don't let that slave catcher see your necklace."

Willie

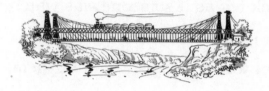

The train stopped. Patrick looked out a small window. The sign above the depot said "Willoughby." He picked up the black bag. Then he opened the side door.

Patrick and Beth hopped off the baggage car and onto the tracks. He heard the door slide shut behind them.

Crowds of people quickly gathered around the back of the train. They cheered for Mr. Lincoln. They were happy and loud. The men and boys wore suits. The women and girls wore dresses with petticoats. Everyone looked as neatly dressed as they would for church.

The cousins glanced at the smoking car that held the reporters.

Patrick felt as if someone was watching him. He looked at the train windows.

A man was staring straight at them. He had red hair and a bushy beard. His forehead was pressed against the glass. But then the man abruptly pulled a shade down.

"Hurry," Beth said. "We might miss Mr. Lincoln."

The people in the crowd yelled, "Speech! Speech!" Their voices rose above the band music coming from the depot.

Patrick turned sideways to squeeze through the crowd. He held the bag over his head to keep from bumping people.

As they reached the back of the train, the

bag was yanked out of his hands. Patrick looked up at a tall man wearing a black stovepipe hat. The man stood on the platform at the rear of the last car. He had a familiar face: the dark hair; the deep-set eyes above a long, bony nose; the sad, thin smile.

"At last," Abraham Lincoln said, "my bag is returned to me. One problem solved." He handed the bag to a young boy in a black suit standing behind him. The boy dropped the bag on the platform.

Then Lincoln leaned over the platform's iron railing and offered Patrick a hand. "Want to come aboard?" Lincoln asked.

Patrick grasped his hand. Mr. Lincoln lifted him to the edge of the platform. Patrick swung a leg over the railing.

I can't believe I'm standing next to Abraham Lincoln, Patrick thought.

"Patrick!" Beth called. "What about me?" She reached up and grabbed two iron rails.

Patrick pulled on Lincoln's sleeve. The tall man looked at Patrick. Patrick pointed to Beth and said, "She helped with the bag too."

This time Lincoln leaned farther over the railing. With two hands, he held Beth around her ribcage and lifted her. Then he gently placed her on the platform.

"Thank you," Beth said. She pushed back her cloak's hood. Then she curtsied to Abraham Lincoln.

The crowd went wild with cheering. The people pressed even closer to the platform and raised their hands toward Lincoln.

The president-elect leaned over the railing again. He shook the hands of men, women, and children.

The other young boy on the platform stepped forward. He cupped his hands around

his mouth. Then he shouted to Lincoln's fans, "Want to meet Mrs. Lincoln?"

The crowd offered more cheers and whistles. The boy pushed Beth to the front of the platform railing.

"Boo!" someone from the crowd said. The cheers turned to jeers and laughter.

The boy laughed so hard he had to hold his stomach.

Beth's cheeks flushed red. She backed away and hid behind a large American flag. It was hanging from a long wood pole. The flag looked odd to Patrick. It had fewer stars than the one at his school.

Lincoln turned to the boy. "Apologize and then go inside, Willie," he said, "and visit Mrs. Lincoln and your younger brother."

"Yes, sir," Willie said. The boy lifted the flag and spoke to Beth. "I was wrong to embarrass you," he said. "But it was a great joke!"

Beth mumbled something that sounded like "Okay." Willie let go of the flag, and Beth was hidden again.

Willie paused before leaving the platform. He said to Patrick, "You look like a fun sort of fellow." Then the boy pulled something out of his pocket. He opened his palm so Patrick could see. "Want to play with my tin soldiers?"

"Uh . . . sure," Patrick said. "Later, though. You should obey Mr. Lincoln."

Willie grinned and went inside.

The train whistle made two long toots. The train began to pull away from the depot. And the locomotive started to chug.

Lincoln said, "Goodbye, friends in Willoughby! I am honored by your loyalty." He turned to Patrick. "Will you be traveling with us to Buffalo? Or are you staying in Willoughby?"

"My ticket was punched for Buffalo," Patrick said.

Several young men raced after the train. They waved small American flags. One raised his arm and hurled something at the platform. Patrick heard a whistle and a loud *ka-bang*!

"A firecracker," Beth said. "How patriotic!"

Patrick looked at Lincoln to share a smile.

But Lincoln had turned pale. "It's time to move inside," he told Patrick and Beth.

Mr. Lincoln picked up the bag and entered the train car.

Patrick was surprised. He looked at Beth. She raised an eyebrow as if to ask, "What's going on?"

Patrick whispered to her, "Perhaps a missing bag wasn't the only problem Mr. Lincoln has."

5

The Lincoln Special

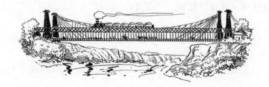

Beth and Patrick followed the future
president inside the train car. This car wasn't
full. It had only a half-dozen men inside.

Beth was surprised to see how fancy it was.
The decor could have been from an expensive
hotel. The fabric on the walls was blue with white
stars. The seat covers were made from red velvet.

The seats were not in rows. Instead they
were arranged like a living room, facing each
other.

Lincoln was so tall he had to hunch over inside the train. He ducked even lower whenever he passed under a light fixture.

"Welcome to the Lincoln Special," Lincoln said. He held his hat in his hands. "Some supporters of mine from Buffalo have provided this train for us. Only my family and special friends are allowed in this car."

Patrick leaned over to Beth. He whispered, "It's like a rolling version of Air Force One, the president's airplane in our time."

Then Patrick asked Mr. Lincoln, "Where's Willie?"

"Mrs. Lincoln has a private compartment in the front of this car," Lincoln said. "My son William is probably there."

Patrick offered his hand to Lincoln. "I'm Patrick," he said. "And this is my cousin Beth. Thank you for letting us visit."

Mr. Lincoln and Patrick shook hands. Then Lincoln bowed to Beth. She curtsied again.

"The thanks is mine," Lincoln said. "My bag has important papers inside. I am grateful it has been found and returned."

Mr. Lincoln motioned for Patrick and Beth to sit on a bench. Patrick took off his wool cloak and folded it. He draped it over the back of his seat.

Beth settled into the comfortable velvet cushion. She felt the warmth of a wood-burning stove in the center of the compartment. The heat fought off the winter chill. But she still pulled her cloak tightly around her.

Mr. Lincoln sat on a similar bench across from them. The black bag was on the floor near him. He put his tall hat on the seat next to him. He pulled a brown blanket across his shoulders.

Mr. Lincoln's long legs stretched out and

filled the space between the benches. He closed his eyes.

Beth pulled in her feet so Lincoln's legs had enough room.

The man who sat directly behind the future president stood up. He had silver hair. His navy-blue suit jacket was so long it almost reached his knees. The jacket had gold buttons down the front of it. The man reached for Lincoln's black bag.

Without opening his eyes, Lincoln said, "Touch that bag, Mr. Wood, and I'll personally put you off the train."

"Just need to check it for security," he said. "Someone left a package for you in Indianapolis. Rumor says it was a bomb." Wood sat back down.

"A bomb!" Beth said. "Do the people in the South hate him so much?" Beth thought of Holman Jones and his goal to enslave

Sally again. He probably didn't like Lincoln much.

Wood turned in his seat so he could answer. He said, "You saw people from the North cheering. They love him! But in the South it's a different story. Seven states have already banded together to leave the Union. They call themselves the Confederate States of America."

"Are the Confederates afraid Mr. Lincoln will end slavery?" Patrick asked.

Wood raised a finger and gestured at Patrick. "Exactly, young man," Wood said. "They will go to war rather than set their slaves free."

Patrick asked, "You mean the Civil War?"

Mr. Lincoln opened his eyes and spoke: "I will do everything in my power to prevent a war between the states. My main goal in this struggle is to save the Union. And stand by my convictions."

The men in the car made noises of approval.

Wood said, "Hear, hear. No one wants such a war."

"And I don't want to see Mr. Lincoln hurt!" Beth said. "He needs to lead the country so that people can be free." *Especially Sally,* she thought.

Beth stood and stepped toward Lincoln. She took his hand. "It's safe inside this train, isn't it?" she asked. "Surely your friends will protect you."

Mr. Lincoln smiled. "Thank you, Beth," he said. "But I'm public property now. I belong to the people who elected me." He squeezed her hand and let it go. "I fully intend to meet as many people as possible. Your compassion is needed more elsewhere."

"Elsewhere?" Beth asked.

"With Mrs. Lincoln," he said. "She isn't feeling well. And the nursemaid who was supposed to care for my son Tad fell ill. She stayed in Illinois."

"Isn't Willie there?" Beth asked.

Mr. Lincoln nodded. "That brings something else to mind," the future president said. "Patrick's helpful nature is needed to distract Willie from troublemaking. Mr. Wood will escort you."

Wood stood and stepped into the aisle. Beth and Patrick followed him toward the front of the car.

Wood opened a door.

Willie's voice called out from inside, "I don't want to take a nap!"

Mrs. Lincoln

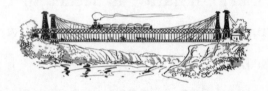

Wood, Beth, and Patrick entered the family section of the train car. It was like a small sitting room. The windows were covered with velvet curtains. Two large wood trunks sat against one wall.

Mary Lincoln sat on a small couch. She smiled at the cousins.

"Thank goodness you're here," Mrs. Lincoln said. "I can't do a thing with Willie."

"I brought Willie a playmate," Wood said.

"And Mr. Lincoln has sent you a nursemaid for Tad. Goodbye, Mrs. Lincoln." He bowed and quickly left.

Willie asked Patrick, "Want to play with my toy soldiers?"

The boys sat on the floor. Willie pulled a handful of Revolutionary War fighters out of his pocket.

Mrs. Lincoln looked at Beth. "Child, that green dress and cloak are fabulous!" Mrs. Lincoln said. "Are they French?"

Beth curtsied and smoothed her

skirt. She said, "I don't know." She took off
her cloak and placed it on a seat, then sat
down.

The future First Lady was also wearing a
lovely dress. It was deep red with a high collar
and short sleeves. The skirt had even more
petticoat fluff than Beth's did.

Beth said, "I think your dress is beautiful too."

"Thank you, dear," Mrs. Lincoln said.

Beth caught movement out of the corner of
her eye. A young boy was on a bed tucked just
under the ceiling. He was peeking out from
beneath a red-and-white-striped blanket.

Beth smiled at him and waved.

Mrs. Lincoln went on, "I wanted to go
shopping for fashionable clothes last week.
But Mr. Wood said I was needed here."

"Don't you want to be with Mr. Lincoln?"
Beth asked.

Mrs. Lincoln put her hands up. "Not on

this train," she said. "The women in the North despise me. They think I'm a country girl because I was born and grew up in the South."

"Then the people in the South must like you," Beth said.

Mrs. Lincoln said, "Southerners despise me because I believe slavery is wrong. The Union is doomed!" The future First Lady lay on the couch. The conversation was over.

Beth saw an ABC picture book on top of a trunk. She lured Tad off the bunk with it. The young boy snuggled next to her on the seat. He was missing his front teeth. Beth guessed he was seven years old.

She read the book a few times in a soft voice.

The train slowed to a stop as the brakes squealed.

Thud!

That noise was followed by banging sounds coming from the train's roof. Beth looked up at the ceiling. It was shaking. The crystal light fixtures were swinging. In an instant, the entire car began to rock.

Tad asked, "What's that noise?"

Mrs. Lincoln stood and rushed to the window. "It's a mob!" she cried. "They've surrounded the train!"

Willie shouted, "Finally, something fun!" He scooped up his soldiers. Then he shoved them into one of his

pants pockets. He stood and rushed out
the door.

"Come back!" Mrs. Lincoln called. But Willie
didn't obey. She turned to Patrick and said,
"Young man, go find Willie."

"Yes, ma'am," Patrick said. He nodded to
Beth and left the compartment.

Outside, excited voices began cheering for
Mr. Lincoln. A band started to play. Several
more thuds came from the ceiling.

Beth feared the roof would cave in. She
gently hugged Tad to comfort him.

Tad pulled on the ribbon that was around
her neck. The wood disk fell on the outside of
Beth's dress.

She let him go and said, "Sit under the
upper bunk. You'll be safer there."

Tad quickly obeyed.

Beth turned around.

Mrs. Lincoln looked shocked. "Where did

you get that necklace?" she asked. The future First Lady stood and came near Beth. The crowds and the noises on the roof seemed forgotten. "Why didn't you tell me?"

"Tell you what?" Beth asked.

"That you're part of the Underground Railroad," Mrs. Lincoln whispered.

That's what Sally said when she saw the necklace! Beth thought. "But I'm not a part of anything," she said.

The woman smiled. Beth could tell Mrs. Lincoln didn't believe her.

"You're a bit young to be involved," Mrs. Lincoln said. "But these are desperate times." She reached for the wood disk. "May I hold it?"

Beth took the necklace off and handed it to Mrs. Lincoln.

"I haven't seen one of these ribbons since I left Kentucky. That was more than twenty years ago," the future First Lady said. "I gave it to Mammy Sally. She was a slave my father owned while I was growing up. I loved her."

Beth's heart leaped. *The runaway slave's name is Sally too*, she thought.

"Mammy Sally gave food and clothing to runaway slaves," Mrs. Lincoln said. "She was brave. I always wondered why she didn't leave too."

"What about the wood disk?" Beth asked. "What does it mean?"

"The goose is a symbol of freedom," Mrs. Lincoln said. "It also means to keep going north toward Canada. Runaways follow geese flying north in the summer."

Mrs. Lincoln slipped the necklace back over Beth's head.

"The schedule for the Lincoln Special is in the newspapers," Mrs. Lincoln said. "And many eyes watch Mr. Lincoln's every move.

A slave on this train would need to be extra careful."

The future First Lady paused. She put a hand on Beth's forearm. "And be careful yourself," she said. "Trust no one."

Lunch

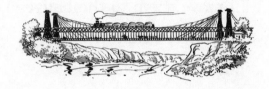

The train began to roll again.

"May I come out now?" Tad asked politely. The boy was still sitting on the narrow bed under the upper bunk. He was wrapped in his blanket.

Mrs. Lincoln moved to him and patted him on the head. She said, "Yes, dear. You were brave during all that racket. But the pounding has stopped now."

Just then Conductor Nottingham came

through the train car door. He held a large basket in his arms. The basket was full of apples and pears and loaves of bread.

He nodded at Mrs. Lincoln and said, "Good day." Then he paused. "I see your trunks are still here. I'll move them to the baggage car. I just have to deliver lunch first."

"Very good," Mrs. Lincoln said.

Baggage car? Beth thought. *He might find Sally. I have to warn her.*

Conductor Nottingham said to Mrs. Lincoln, "Would you like your lunch here or in the main section?"

"We will dine with Mr. Lincoln," she said.

Nottingham hurried to Mr. Lincoln's section of the car.

Mrs. Lincoln went to one of the wood trunks. She took out a hand mirror and looked at herself. She arranged her smooth brown hair and then put the mirror back.

The future First Lady took Tad by the
hand. "Beth," she said, "we will dine with Mr.
Lincoln now."

Patrick was seated near the stove with Willie.
They were eating lunch. Patrick had a large,
white, cloth napkin on his lap. The napkin had
apple slices, cheese, and a chunk of bread on it.
Patrick also had a glass of lemonade.

Patrick watched Beth come in with Mrs.
Lincoln and Tad.

Wood and the other men in the car stood.
Patrick guessed it was to honor the future
First Lady. So he wrapped the food up in his
napkin. He quickly slurped the lemonade and
set the glass on the floor. Then he and Willie
stood too.

Mrs. Lincoln moved to an open seat near
Mr. Lincoln. She sat down.

Patrick, Willie, and the men sat down again, except for Conductor Nottingham. He prepared more food and lemonade and offered it to Mrs. Lincoln.

Beth and Tad walked over to the seats near the stove.

Tad sat next to Willie. The two brothers started whispering to each other.

Beth sat next to Patrick. She said quietly, "We've got a problem."

"What's wrong?" Patrick asked.

But Beth didn't have a chance to answer. Conductor Nottingham was standing right next to her. A basket of food hung on his arm, and he held a glass of lemonade in each hand.

"Would you care for some apples and lemonade?" he asked Beth and Tad.

They each took the offered food and thanked the conductor.

"Apples are my favorite!" Tad said. "Thank you." He bit into a slice.

The conductor looked at Mr. Lincoln and said, "The engineer received a telegram from the Buffalo depot. Crowds have already filled the train station. Thousands more people are on their way."

Mr. Lincoln chuckled. "This is a government of the people, by the people, and for the people," he said. "Let them come."

"Confound it!" Wood said angrily. "What's to be done to protect you? You're determined to put yourself at the mercy of mobs. The train roof could have caved in."

"Not to worry," Nottingham said. "The governor of New York has police and soldiers to help in Buffalo. They will escort Mr. Lincoln from the train to the American Hotel."

Mr. Lincoln's black bag was on the floor next to him. Nottingham motioned to it with his foot. He said, "The less you have to carry when you leave the train, the better. I'm taking Mrs. Lincoln's trunks to the baggage car. I'd like to bring this bag also."

Patrick looked at Beth. Her forehead was scrunched with worry lines. She whispered, "*That's* the problem. What about Sally?"

Patrick handed his napkin and glass to Beth. Then he jumped up.

Willie did the same.

"I'll take the bag," Patrick said. "It's my job. That and to keep Willie out of trouble."

He spoke to Mrs. Lincoln. "I'll take your trunks, too. I'm sure Conductor Nottingham has more important things to do." He gave a little bow.

"That's the spirit," Wood said. "A young man who likes responsibility."

Nottingham said, "Thank you, young man.
But I don't think you're strong enough to
carry the trunks."

Mr. Lincoln reached down and picked up
his bag. He opened it and took out a few
papers. He tucked them inside his hat. "That's
my inaugural speech," he said. "I can't lose it
again. But you may take the bag now,
thank you."

Patrick picked up the bag. "I'll put
this back in the baggage car," he said.

Wood said, "And make sure you
keep the baggage car locked. The crowds are
getting bolder. Someone may try to get inside
that car and steal something."

"Or worse," Lincoln said. "Someone might
get a free ride to Buffalo!"

Someone like Sally, Patrick thought. "I'll
need the key from Conductor Nottingham,
then," he said.

"I usually don't do this," the conductor said. He reached into his jacket pocket. He pulled out a bundle and took one long key off the ring. "It's against railroad policy to hand these out. But since you're working for the president-elect . . ."

Willie snatched the key out of the conductor's hand. "We'll wait for you to come with the trunks," Willie said.

"*We?*" Patrick asked. "You're coming with me?"

Willie beamed a smile. "Yes," he said. "I want to learn responsibility." Willie kissed his mother's cheek goodbye.

"I'm proud of you," Lincoln said. He patted Willie on the head.

Then Willie ran to the compartment door. "Come on, Patrick," he said. "Let's go!"

Patrick felt as if he had no choice. He carried the bag out the door.

The Trunks

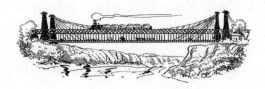

Beth's heart was racing. *What will Patrick do if Willie sees Sally?* she wondered. Beth thought of a plan to help Patrick. She moved Tad away from the stove to sit nearer the Lincolns.

Tad gulped his lemonade.

Nottingham took Tad's empty glass. Then he arranged the rest of the fruit in the basket. He left it on a seat that also held a stack of newspapers.

Nottingham bowed to the future First Lady. He said, "I'll take your trunks to the baggage car now, ma'am."

Beth asked Mrs. Lincoln, "Don't you need to change your dress first?"

"No, no," Mrs. Lincoln said. She quickly shook her head. "This is the gown I've chosen for the people in Buffalo. It will be the largest crowd yet."

Mrs. Lincoln turned to her husband. "Don't I look beautiful?" she asked.

Mr. Lincoln smiled and patted her hand. "The dress shows off your lovely complexion and clear blue eyes," he said.

Beth pulled out the necklace from beneath her dress. She fingered it so Mrs. Lincoln could see it.

She said, "But wouldn't a *goose* feather shawl look more fashionable?"

Mrs. Lincoln seemed to perk up. She looked at Beth. "Yes," she said cheerfully. "I think you're right. *Goose* feathers are all the rage. Let's go find something for me to wear in the evening. It'll take me just a minute."

WANTED

Isobel Culver, also known as "Sally"

Reward $450

for information leading to her capture.

Light brown skin. Intelligent expression.

Brand on her left shoulder.

The conductor sat down. "I'll get the sack truck, then," he said.

The future First Lady stood. "Beth," she said, "please bring Tad and the fruit. I'm still hungry."

Beth grabbed the fruit basket off the seat. Then she followed Mrs. Lincoln and Tad into the family area.

Mary Todd Lincoln shut the door. She turned to Beth. "You have a runaway in the baggage compartment, don't you?" Mrs. Lincoln whispered.

Beth nodded and whispered back, "She'll be discovered soon!"

● ● ●

Patrick and Willie hurried through the smoking car. Patrick plugged his nose. He didn't want to breathe the smoke.

Holman Jones was talking to several men near the front of the car. One of them was the reporter with the red hair and thick beard.

The slave catcher saw Patrick and waved the poster at him. Patrick looked at the ground as he walked past. He didn't want to say anything to Jones.

Patrick and Willie arrived at the baggage car. Willie unlocked the door. The boys went in and closed the door behind them.

"So where's the slave?" Willie asked suddenly.

Patrick felt as if he'd been kicked in the stomach. *How did Willie know?* he wondered.

Willie sat on a suitcase as if he were glued there. He folded his arms.

"Tad told me you and Beth are with the Underground Railroad," Willie said. "He heard our mother say so. Beth has a special necklace."

Patrick put the black bag down. He said, "We're not with anything. I think it's time to go."

"Not before I see the slave," Willie said. "One is in here, right?"

"Yes, one is." It was Sally's muffled voice.

Willie jumped up. "I knew it!" he cried. He climbed the stack of trunks. Then he moved the carpetbag covering her hiding place.

"I'm William Wallace Lincoln," he said. "My

father is going to be president. I've heard him say he hates slavery."

"Good for him," Sally said. "I hate slavery too."

● ● ●

Mrs. Lincoln opened both of the cedar trunks. She repacked all the contents from one trunk into the other. "Is Sally tall?" the future First Lady asked.

"She's a teenager and very thin," Beth said. "It's possible she can fit in here."

"Good," Mrs. Lincoln said. She tried to close the packed trunk, but it was too full.

She took out a feather shawl and a blue cloak with a hood. Then she sat on the trunk lid. It closed. Mrs. Lincoln locked it.

"Mother, will Sally be able to breathe in there?" Tad asked.

The Mistake

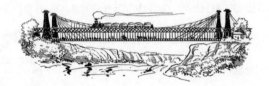

Mrs. Lincoln stood up from the trunk. "We're trying to keep Sally away from the slave catcher," she said. "We're not trying to suffocate her."

Mrs. Lincoln put the blue cloak inside the nearly empty trunk. She slipped something inside the cloak pocket. "That's for Sally," she said. She closed the lid.

Sally's not going inside it? Beth wondered. *What is the trunk for?*

Beth heard heavy footsteps and then Conductor Nottingham's voice. "I've brought the sack truck."

The sack truck was a tall, narrow cart with two wheels. It looked like something Whit would use to move heavy boxes or appliances.

"You will take that one first," Mrs. Lincoln said. She pointed to the empty trunk.

Conductor Nottingham nodded to Mrs. Lincoln. "Yes, ma'am," he said. Then he loaded the trunk onto the sack truck. "This one feels almost empty," the conductor said.

"That's my business," the future First Lady said.

"But—" he started to say.

"Not a word, Conductor," Mrs. Lincoln said sternly. *"Not one word."*

Nottingham nodded. He used thick leather belts to strap the trunk to the cart. Nottingham started to whistle as he left the compartment. The trunk bumped the doorframe on the way out.

Mrs. Lincoln turned to Beth. She put her hands on her hips. "What are you waiting for?" she asked.

"Me?" Beth said.

"You," Mrs. Lincoln said. "Pick up that food basket and skedaddle. Follow the conductor."

"Then what?" Beth asked.

Mrs. Lincoln leaned over and whispered in Beth's ear.

"Got it!" Beth said. Then she grinned so

wide her cheeks hurt. *That'll fix Holman
Jones*, she thought.

Beth gave Tad a quick hug goodbye. Then
she grabbed her own green cloak and put it
on. She picked up the basket and hurried
after Conductor Nottingham.

Beth caught up with him in the smoking car.

The slave catcher was blocking the aisle.
Next to him stood a man in a brown suit. He
had red hair and a thick beard. He was taking
notes on a small pad of paper. Beth guessed
he was a reporter.

Beth wanted to hang back or go around the
men. But Mrs. Lincoln had given her a job.
She neared the trunk and set the basket on
top of it.

The trunk shifted slightly.

"That's odd," the red-haired man said. "How
can a half-empty basket move a wood trunk
with just a nudge?"

Jones rapped his knuckles on the trunk. It made a deep, hollow thump. "Sounds empty to me," Jones said to Nottingham. "What's inside?"

"Mind your own business," Nottingham said.

Jones sneered. "It *is* my business," he said. "This trunk looks like the perfect size to hide a runaway slave."

Jones opened one side of his long leather coat. He revealed the revolver and the whip.

Beth's eyes grew round with fear. She held in a gasp.

"Let me look inside the trunk," Jones said. He patted the star-shaped badge on his jacket. "The law is on my side. No one can stop me from searching for runaways."

"You're going to shoot me to look inside Mrs. Lincoln's trunk?" the conductor asked. He shook his head as if to say Jones wasn't very smart. Then Nottingham said in a serious tone, "You said yourself the trunk is empty. Let me pass."

"With pleasure," Jones said.

Beth picked up the basket off the trunk.

Jones closed his jacket. Then he stepped out of the aisle. Nottingham pushed the sack truck toward the baggage car door.

Jones suddenly blocked the aisle again. This time he stopped Beth's passage. "But not you!" Jones said.

"Why not?" Beth asked. "Do you think a slave is hiding in this basket?"

He smiled, but not nicely. "Very funny," he said. "There's no slave in the trunk. But you'd better explain why you're taking food into the baggage car. *And* why you're wearing a trinket from the Underground Railroad. Sally wore a necklace just like it."

This time Beth did gasp. One of her hands flew to her necklace. She'd forgotten to hide it underneath her dress. *Oh no!* she thought. *Holman Jones saw the goose!*

Patrick stood guard at the baggage car door. He didn't want anyone to come in and find Sally. Sally was inside her hideaway. Willie stood on top of the stack of luggage. He was talking to Sally in a hushed voice.

Patrick expected Mrs. Lincoln's trunks to come soon. He opened the door a crack and peeked out.

He saw Conductor Nottingham pulling a cart across the connecting platform. Patrick shut the door. He whispered over his shoulder to Willie and Sally, "Conductor Nottingham is coming."

Sally said, "Quick, Willie. Get off the luggage! But put the carpetbag back on top first!"

Willie moved the flowered carpetbag to cover Sally's hideaway. Then he leaped from the stack of luggage and landed with a thud.

Just then Conductor Nottingham opened the door. "Come here, lad," he said to Patrick. "Help me unstrap Mrs. Lincoln's trunk."

Patrick unbuckled the leather belt.

The conductor picked up the trunk as if it were a pillow.

"Is it empty?" Patrick asked.

"That's not my business," the conductor said. He placed the trunk near the others. "Leastwise that's what Mrs. Lincoln tells me." He winked at Patrick and then chuckled.

The train's whistle blasted two long notes. The train slowed to a stop.

"That's my cue to leave," the conductor said. "I'll have my key back."

Willie handed Nottingham the key. "I didn't lose it," he said. "Was I responsible?"

"Very," the conductor said. He slipped the key into his pocket.

Nottingham opened the wide door on the side of the car.

Patrick felt a gust of cold air enter the train.

"It's time that I get off," Nottingham said. "This is my last stop. A new conductor is coming. He'll have to move Mrs. Lincoln's second trunk. And he'll arrange the bags for unloading at Buffalo."

Nottingham stepped off the train. He stood on the ground, looking inside the baggage car. He said, "Your young friend is coming in just a minute. She's in the smoking car talking to that mean fellow. He was mighty interested in something she was wearing."

Willie slid the door closed.

Patrick gulped. *The necklace!* he thought.

The Whip Cracks

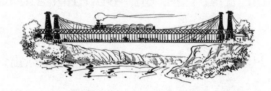

Beth backed away from the slave catcher. "It's just a necklace my friend gave me," she said. "It means nothing."

Jones sneered. He poked the necklace with his index finger. "Nothing?" he said. "It's a symbol telling slaves that it's safe. But no slave is safe when I'm around."

Beth lifted her chin. She wanted to act as Mrs. Lincoln would, like a queen. "I'm nursemaid to Tad Lincoln," Beth said. "And Mrs. Lincoln will be angry if you bother me."

The reporter wrote down something on his notepad. "What's your name?" he asked. "The *Cincinnati Daily Press* pays me to get all the details."

"Let me pass," Beth said.

Suddenly Holman Jones laughed. He motioned with his arm for Beth to go down the aisle.

Beth tucked the necklace under her dress. She hurried out the door toward the baggage car.

The train whistle blew twice as she crossed the connecting platform.

The trap is set, Beth thought. *Will Jones step into it?*

● ● ●

Patrick saw Beth and flung the door wide open.

Beth hurried in and shut the door behind her. "Can we lock the door?" she asked.

"No," Patrick said. "We don't have the key anymore."

Beth leaned against the door and took a deep breath.

"Holman Jones will be here any second," Beth said.

"But he'll find Sally," Willie said.

"No, he won't," Beth said. "He's too smart."

Patrick was confused. "If Jones is so smart," he said, "he'll find Sally for sure."

"There's no time to explain," Beth said. "Just keep Jones out till I say to let him in."

Beth said so Sally could hear, "Pray like you've never prayed before."

Patrick heard someone outside on the connecting platform. He leaned against the door with all his might.

Willie did too.

There was a knock on the door.

"Let me in." It was Jones's voice. "I demand

to search the baggage car. I have a legal right to do it."

Patrick looked at Beth. She opened the trunk. Then she took out the blue cloak and laid it on a crate. Next she emptied the fruit basket inside the trunk. Then she slammed the lid closed.

Beth started dragging Mrs. Lincoln's trunk toward the side door. "Just a little bit more time," she said.

Patrick felt Willie's body shift. The boy reached into his pocket for a tin soldier. Then he wedged it between the door and the side post. Only the little man's feet were sticking out.

"That should hold it," Willie said. Then he rushed to open the side door.

Beth pushed the trunk to the edge.

Patrick had no idea what Willie and Beth were doing.

Jones jiggled the doorknob. But the toy soldier was still holding as a wedge. Still Patrick kept leaning against the door just in case.

Bam. Bam. Bam. Jones's fist hit the door. "Sally is in there," the slave catcher shouted, "and I will catch her. Then I'll beat her unless you open the door!"

Help us, God, Beth prayed.

A railroad man on the depot platform walked past the open side door. "I'll help you with that," he said. The man lifted the trunk off the train. He set it on the depot platform.

Beth said, "Thank you."

"Who's in charge of this trunk?" the man asked.

"A man will come looking for it in a minute," Beth said. "He's blond and wearing a long, leather coat."

The railroad worker lifted his hat at Beth. "All right, then," he said. "Have a good day."

Willie moved to the sliding door and slammed it shut. "Are we ready?" he asked.

"Yes," Beth said.

Beth heard a squeaking sound. The brakes on the train released. Any second the train would begin to move away from the depot.

"Take out the toy soldier," Willie called to Patrick.

Beth took Willie's arm. The two of them moved to the center of the baggage car.

Beth watched as Patrick pulled the toy soldier from the doorframe. Then he joined Beth and Willie.

Jones burst through the door. His whip was in his hand. He cracked the long, leather strap in the air. *Snap.*

It sounded like a gunshot. Beth flinched.

"Where is Sally?" Jones asked. His voice sounded like an animal's growl. He snapped the whip again.

The children were silent. Beth felt sweat dripping down her neck. Her hands began to sweat. She was so afraid she couldn't speak. She held Willie's and Patrick's hands. Their hands were damp too.

The slave catcher moved his head from side to side. He was searching for Sally. "There's the basket," he said. "But where's the food?" He turned around. "And where's the trunk?"

The train started moving. The familiar clacking sound gave Beth courage.

She said, "You're too late."

Jones scowled when he heard her. "No!" he said. He cracked the whip in anger. *Snap!*

Beth felt a rush of air near her ear. The tip of the whip just missed her.

The slave catcher rushed to the side door and slid it open. He stuck his head outside. Light flooded the baggage car. Voices from people on the platform were shouting goodbye to the Lincoln Special.

"The trunk!" Jones shouted. "Sally and the food must be inside!"

Jones looked over his shoulder at Beth. "I win," the slave catcher said.

Then Jones leaped off the rolling train.

The Tickets

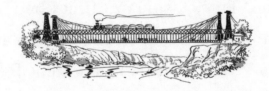

Patrick moved first. He closed the sliding door.

"*We* win! Jones is gone!" Willie said. "Hurrah!"

The flowered carpetbag fell to the floor. Sally slowly climbed out of her hideaway.

"You don't look well," Patrick said. He went to help Sally down. He clasped her hand in his as she stepped over the luggage. Patrick felt her small hand trembling.

Beth hurried to Sally's side. She wrapped Mrs. Lincoln's blue cloak around Sally.

"Poor girl," Beth said. "You must have been so scared when you heard Jones's whip snap. I didn't have time to tell you about the plan."

"Or me," Patrick said. "At first I had no idea why you put the trunk on the depot platform."

"Sorry," Beth said. "I'm glad Willie figured it out and helped me."

"I thought I was caught," Sally said. She wiped tears from her cheeks. "I thought I had to go back."

Beth put her arm around Sally's shoulders.

"You're safe now," Patrick said. That only made Sally begin to sob.

"I won't . . . be . . . safe . . ." she said between breaths, "until . . . I'm . . . in . . . Canada."

Beth squeezed Sally's shoulders in a gentle hug. Sally leaned into her, and they both cried.

Patrick backed away. Crying girls made him uncomfortable.

Willie followed him.

Patrick whispered, "We have a new conductor now. He's going to rearrange the luggage."

Willie said, "I think we should take Sally to Mrs. Lincoln. She'll make sure Sally is safe."

Patrick said, "Will Sally need a ticket when the new conductor comes aboard?" He reached inside his pocket and fingered the single ticket. "I have an extra, but it's for a ferry in Buffalo."

"A ticket won't matter if she's with my mother," Willie said. Then he called to the girls, "Wipe your tears. It's time to go."

Patrick whistled. He said to Willie, "You *are* responsible."

Willie smiled and then said, "Don't tell Wood. He'd make me help. I'd rather do pranks, because they make Mr. Lincoln smile." He gave Patrick a playful punch in the arm.

"We're ready," Beth said. The girls were holding hands.

Patrick said, "People have seen Jones's poster. We have to try to keep Sally's face hidden."

WANTED

Isobel Culver, also known as "Sally"

Reward $450

for information leading to her capture.

Light brown skin. Intelligent expression.

Brand on her left shoulder.

Beth released Sally's hand and pulled up her own hood. Then she helped Sally pull the blue hood over her head. It was big enough to cover most of her face.

Patrick led the way out of the baggage car. They followed him across the connecting platform. They all entered the smoking car. He was for once glad of the smoky haze. It would make Sally's face even harder to see.

Sally followed Patrick down the center aisle, keeping her head low. Beth and Willie were not far behind.

Patrick glanced around the car. No one paid attention to them except the red-haired, bearded man. He stood near the stove in the center of the train car.

As Patrick passed, the red-haired man smiled. He motioned for the children to stop.

Patrick slowed and said, "We're in a hurry."

"This will take just a moment," the man said politely. "I'm Hal Ross from the *Cincinnati Daily Press*. I'd like to meet Mr. Lincoln. Perhaps you can help me."

Patrick relaxed a little. The reporter probably just wanted news about President-elect Lincoln.

Ross took out a small pad of paper from his pocket. "Let's start with the details. The girl in the green is Tad Lincoln's nursemaid," Ross said. "But who are the rest of you?" He pointed to Sally with his pencil. "Especially the girl in blue."

Patrick heard Sally inhale quickly. She kept her head lowered so the hood hid her face.

Suddenly Willie said to Ross, "Want to meet Mr. Lincoln?"

The reporter moved toward Willie. Ross's face wore an eager grin. "Can you get me in to see Mr. Lincoln?" he asked.

Willie put one foot forward and raised his arms. He waved his palms. "Ta-dah! I'm Mr. Lincoln!" he said. "William Wallace Lincoln, that is!"

Ross wasn't watching Sally anymore. Patrick smiled at Willie's joke. For once, Willie's silliness was helpful. Patrick guided Sally away from Ross and toward the door.

Just then an unfamiliar man entered the smoking car. He wore a three-piece blue suit and a conductor's hat. He was pushing Mrs. Lincoln's second trunk with a little cart.

"I'm Conductor Morehead, representing the Buffalo and Erie Railroad Company," he shouted. "Tickets out, please!"

Beth was right behind Sally and Patrick. She heard the conductor's words, and her heart fluttered. *Sally doesn't have a ticket. He'll put her off the train.*

Beth quickly stepped toward Conductor Morehead to distract him from Sally. She reached into her cloak pocket and held out her ticket. "I'm punched all the way to Buffalo," she said.

The new conductor took Beth's ticket and inspected it. He punched the ticket again and handed it back to her. He smiled and said, "Thank you."

Then Conductor Morehead stepped farther into the car, pushing the cart away from the door. He approached Ross. "Excuse me," he said, "but I need to see your ticket."

Ross shook his notepad. His ticket dropped out, and he handed it to the conductor. The conductor punched the ticket and returned it.

Patrick was next. He reached in his pocket and pulled out a ticket.

"This one is for the Black Rock Ferry," said Morehead.

"Oh?" Ross said. "Are you going to Canada on the ferry?" He held the pencil over the notepad. "And is Mr. William Lincoln going with you?"

Beth looked to Willie to see how he would answer. But the boy was gone. And so was Sally!

Grace Bedell

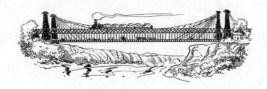

Patrick handed Conductor Morehead his other ticket. Then he put the first one back in his pocket. "Everything is in order," Morehead said after punching Patrick's train ticket.

The conductor pulled a pocket watch out of his vest. "It's one thirty. We have only five minutes before we reach North East station," he said. "I need to punch everyone's ticket on this car before that. And I need to put this trunk in the baggage car."

The conductor snapped his watch closed and returned it to his vest. He lifted his hat to Beth.

Beth smiled. "Thank you, sir," she said.

The conductor pushed the trunk toward the baggage car.

Patrick had almost forgotten about Ross.

"A word, sir?" Ross said to the new conductor. "Will the stop at North East station be long? I want go into the depot and wire a message."

"You'll have time if you hurry," the conductor said.

"Right," said Ross. He wrote something on his notepad. "Thank you."

Beth gently nudged Patrick with her elbow. "Let's go," she said. The cousins turned toward the rear of the train.

Beth and Patrick entered Mr. Lincoln's train car. Patrick paused. "I'm going to find Willie,"

he said. Patrick headed to the back of the train.

Beth moved inside Mrs. Lincoln's compartment. She felt safer there.

It seemed Sally did too. The runaway was sitting on a seat. The blue cloak was draped over the back of it. Tad sat next to her. The young boy was reading the ABC book to her.

Mrs. Lincoln was looking on and smiling. When Beth caught her eye, Mrs. Lincoln gave her a wink.

The train whistle blasted twice. Beth felt the train slow.

Beth picked up a newspaper. The front page had the schedule for the Lincoln Special.

"The train has a few more stops," she told Sally. "North East, Westfield, Dunkirk, and Silver Creek. It's due in Buffalo at five o'clock. Only about three more hours."

The train slowed and stopped.

Willie looked out the window. "This is the depot in North East," he said. "There's only a small crowd. Mr. Lincoln won't get out."

A few minutes later, the train whistle blew. Beth felt relieved. They were closer to Buffalo with each stop.

Patrick and Willie were playing with the tin soldiers near the stove again.

Patrick was glad to see the one Willie had employed as a wedge. It was dented but still usable. The little man looked battle-worthy.

The train whistle blew one long toot. The noise caused the men sitting near Lincoln to stir.

"This must be Westfield," Lincoln said in a hoarse voice. "I've been looking forward to this stop."

Wood stood and began pacing. "No need to talk so much here," he said. "Your voice will fail if you're not quiet. Save your vocal cords for the people of Buffalo."

"I have a special friend here," Lincoln said. "I will address the crowd." He rose from his seat and picked up his black hat. Then he ducked and stepped through the rear door and onto the platform.

Willie put the tin soldiers in his pocket. Then he and Patrick joined Lincoln on the back platform.

Lincoln was waving to the large crowd.

The people were cheering and clapping. Everyone wore nice clothes. Patrick was amazed that ladies would crowd closely together in their wide, fluffy dresses.

Lincoln said loudly, "I am glad to see you. I suppose you are glad to see me."

The crowd went wild with cheers and claps. Women waved handkerchiefs. Men waved hats and American flags.

Lincoln continued, "But you folks are so good looking. It seems I have the best of the bargain."

The crowd laughed. Then they clapped again.

Lincoln said, "Three months ago, a young lady mailed me a letter. Her name is Grace Bedell. She suggested I let my whiskers grow to improve my looks."

Lincoln raised his hand to stroke his scraggly beard.

A young lad sitting on a nearby post pointed toward the back of the crowd and said, "There's Grace!"

The crowd parted. A young girl walked toward the train platform. She carried a bouquet of roses in her arms.

Patrick thought she looked about eleven years old.

The crowd moved away from the platform railing. Grace climbed the steep steps to the platform. Lincoln stepped toward her.

The crowd cheered. Grace and Lincoln spoke to each other softly.

Patrick was too far away to hear what they said.

Then Lincoln shook Grace's hand. He gave her a swift, gentle kiss on the cheek.

Grace smiled sweetly and blushed as red as a tomato. Then she hurried down the stairs with the flowers. She disappeared into the crowd.

The people began cheering even louder. Lincoln waved to them and then went back into the train car.

Willie giggled. He leaned toward Patrick and whispered, "I'll bet she was nervous. She forgot to give Mr. Lincoln those roses."

The Telegram

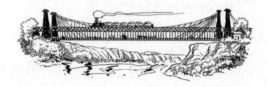

The train whistle blew twice. Patrick left the platform and entered the train car. Conductor Morehead was inside. Lincoln was already relaxed in his seat, blanket on, hat off.

Patrick went to the seat with his cloak draped over the back.

The conductor turned to Wood. "I have a telegram for you," Morehead said. "Two came in at Westfield." He handed Wood a piece of paper.

Wood read the message out loud, "'BR Ferry watched. On horseback HJ.'" Wood was silent for a few seconds. "Hmm," he said, "That doesn't make any sense." He studied the paper. "It was sent from the Erie depot," he said.

The conductor looked at another paper. "My mistake, sir," he said. "That one is for a reporter. This one is for you."

The conductor and Wood exchanged papers.

Wood scanned the new telegram. "Another message from the New York governor," he said. "Mrs. Lincoln will be given a carriage for her and the children. It will be waiting at the depot."

Willie nudged Patrick. The boys stepped away from the men and toward the stove. "Do you think the first telegram from HJ could mean Holman Jones?" Willie whispered. "But who is BR?"

"Not who. *What* is BR," Patrick said. He pulled the extra ticket from his pocket. "This is a one-way ticket to Canada. It's on the Black Rock Ferry for tonight. That must be the BR Ferry."

"How did Holman Jones know about the ferry?" Willie asked.

Patrick said, "I'll bet that Hal Ross told Jones through a telegram. He wants part of the reward, the fifty silver pieces."

Willie said, "Does 'on horseback' mean Mr. Jones is following the train?"

That thought made Patrick feel cold with dread. "That makes sense," he said. "Jones can probably catch up easily. This train stops so many times."

Wood called to them. "Willie and Patrick," he said, "go tell Mrs. Lincoln about the carriage. And stay in there. We men are going to talk politics."

"Yes, sir," Patrick said. He picked up his cloak and put it on.

"Fine with me," Willie said. "I'm more a man of action than words."

Mr. Lincoln gave a hearty laugh.

Mrs. Lincoln napped with Tad on the lower bunk bed. The four older children had to be quiet. They sat near one another in a cluster of seats.

The train stopped in Dunkirk and Silver Creek, New York. But none of them went out on the platform with President-elect Lincoln. Not even Willie.

After the second stop, Beth asked Sally, "Why did you run away?"

"I was a house slave for a rich Kentucky plantation owner. His name was Benjamin Culver," she said. "Once Mr. Lincoln got elected, many states left the Union. But Kentucky didn't."

Sally sighed. Then she said, "Master Culver feared the slave laws would change in our state. So he decided to send all his slaves to his brother's plantation. His brother lives in South Carolina."

"That doesn't seem fair," Beth said.

"I would be a field worker in South Carolina," Sally said. "I didn't want to go farther south. Kentucky is right on the border between the North and the South. It's much closer to Canada. So I ran."

Patrick told them about the telegram from Jones. He said, "You can't take the ferry across to Canada. Holman Jones will be watching. He's probably riding straight to Buffalo on horseback."

Beth asked, "What will you do when we get to Buffalo?"

"It's a secret," Sally said. "I'll have to find out from the next conductor. He's at the American Hotel. He's a cook named Murray who is a freed slave. That's all I know."

The train whistle blew one long toot. The brakes squealed.

Willie looked out the window. "It's mobbed," he said. "It's ten times the people that have been at other stops."

Mrs. Lincoln rose from the bunk. She picked up a small handbag with beads on it. "Everyone grab your cloaks," she said. "A carriage will take us to the American Hotel."

Sally gasped. "Me too?" she asked.

Mrs. Lincoln said, "Of course. Now hurry up. You may

take the blue cloak. Keep the hood over your face in public. Others may want to collect Mr. Jones's reward."

The children got ready to leave. They waited near the door to the connecting platform. Conductor Morehead was there to help them.

Two railroad men helped Mrs. Lincoln and Sally into the carriage first. Next Tad, and then Willie.

When Beth got to the platform, she could see the crowds behind her. They reminded her of bees in a beehive she had once seen. The worker bees had been trying to get to the queen. But now instead of buzzing, these bees were shouting at one another.

"Quit shoving!" they said. "Where's Lincoln? Has anyone seen him?" and "If you step on my foot again, I'll wallop you."

Beth could now see the carriage. It had two white horses harnessed to the front.

Conductor Morehead helped her into it. "Don't slip," he said. "There's mud everywhere. It snowed yesterday, but it melted this morning."

Beth sat next to Sally. Both girls pulled their cloaks around them to keep away the winter chill.

Patrick jumped in the carriage by himself and sat down. His movement rocked the vehicle. Beth heard the horses stamp their hooves. One of them whinnied.

The carriage driver snapped the harness reins.

Beth felt Sally shudder. The sound probably reminded her of the slave catcher's whip.

"Don't worry," Beth said. "Jones is gone."

The driver snapped the reins again. The horses moved away from the train.

Beth looked back at the Lincoln Special. She could see a red-haired man looking out the window. He was watching them leave in the carriage. It was the reporter Hal Ross.

Murray

The carriage started slowly at first. Soldiers
in blue uniforms cleared a path so the horses
could move.

The horses clomped on till the carriage
moved away from the depot. The crowds were
waving American flags, handkerchiefs, and
hats.

After a few minutes, the driver said,
"That's the hotel over there." He pointed to a
rectangular, block-long building. An American

flag on top of the building fluttered in the breeze.

"My family will be staying here," Willie said. "The governor of New York will throw a party for us. And Mr. Lincoln will give a speech about his convictions."

"I hope to be in Canada by then," Sally said.

The carriage pulled up in front of the hotel. Mrs. Lincoln said, "Please take us around back to the kitchen. I need to speak to a cook named Murray."

The driver did as he was told. The carriage soon stopped in front of a plain, thick door.

The driver said, "I'll get Murray for you."

"Thank you," Mrs. Lincoln said.

The driver wasn't gone long. He came back with a man wearing a white apron. The man was tall and thin. His skin was as dark as chocolate. He wiped his floured hands on his apron.

"What do you want?" he asked. "I'm busy preparing for President Lincoln's party."

"Would you like to meet Mrs. Lincoln?" asked Willie.

The man's eyes grew big as if he'd seen a ghost. "Mrs. Lincoln!" he said.

"Driver, why don't you go to the kitchen for a cup of coffee?" Mrs. Lincoln said. "I need to speak to this man for a few minutes."

When the driver was gone, she turned to Murray. "I require your services," Mrs. Lincoln said simply. "Please help Sally."

Sally lowered her hood. "I've come all the way from Kentucky," she said. She showed him the necklace with the Underground Railroad symbol.

"No runaway should be seen in daylight, ma'am," Murray said to Mrs. Lincoln. "Pardon me, but you'll get her caught. Please come back after dark." His kind, brown eyes were filled with worry.

"We can't," Beth said. "A slave catcher was on the Lincoln Special. His friend saw us leave for the hotel. It won't be long till the slave catcher is here. Sally has to get away *now*."

Murray seemed to think it over. Finally he said, "I'll tell you the way to Black Rock Ferry. You can meet with—"

Willie interrupted. "The ferry is being watched," he said. "A telegram said so."

Murray looked surprised. "That's the next station," he said. "There is no other."

Murray's words made Patrick's heart sink. "There has to be another way," he said.

"There is," Willie said. He leaned close to Mrs. Lincoln. He whispered in her ear. Then Mrs. Lincoln nodded. She motioned for Tad and Willie to get out of the carriage.

The boys got out, and Murray helped
Mrs. Lincoln get down.

"Would a carriage and two horses help?"
the future First Lady asked.

Murray grinned. "It would,"
he said. Murray pulled himself
up into the driver's seat. "I will
take you to Niagara Falls
myself. You can take a train
to Canada from there."

Mrs. Lincoln said,
"I'll talk to your
boss and tell him
I needed you.
That way you
won't get fired
for leaving
your
job."

"Thank you both," Sally said softly.

Mrs. Lincoln looked at Beth and Patrick. She said, "Since you're with the Underground Railroad, I'm sure you'll want to go with them."

The cousins nodded in reply.

"Safe travels," Mrs. Lincoln said. She and Tad waved goodbye.

"You'll be the prettiest woman at tonight's party," Beth said to Mrs. Lincoln. "Thank you for all your help."

Patrick said, "I hope we meet again!"

"I do too," Willie said. "You all are loads of fun and adventure."

Murray turned around to face the children. "I know who Sally is, but who are you two?"

"I'm Patrick," he said. "And this is my cousin Beth."

"We're taking the long way around to the Niagara River," Murray said. "It will take all night. The way has narrow country roads, hills, trees, and mud. No bridges and no ferries."

"And no slave catchers," Sally said.

The children sat quietly as Murray drove them all away. Patrick heard the sounds of the crowd in the distance. People were cheering. A cannon fired. Somewhere a band was playing "The Star-Spangled Banner." Patrick strained his ears for sounds of danger.

Murray steered the carriage to a dirt road. It took them away from the city. The horses pulled the carriage up a hill. It pitched slowly from side to side. The horses' hooves squished in the mud. The sounds of the city grew quieter with each turn of the wheels.

Beth and Sally leaned against each other. Sally closed her eyes, and her breathing slowed.

Beth nodded off too.

Patrick looked at the sky. The sun sat on the horizon like a giant yellow button. He closed his eyes, just for a moment . . .

"We're here!"

Patrick jolted awake at the sound of Murray's voice.

Niagara Falls

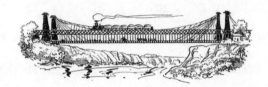

Niagara Falls sounded like a mighty rush of wind combined with a lion's roar. The air was thick with mist. The rising sun cast a warm glow over the tree trunks and rocky ground.

Beth sat upright and pulled her green cloak tightly around her. She smiled at Patrick. He rubbed his eyes.

Murray stood next to the carriage. He patted the nose of one of the horses. "Up ahead is our newfangled bridge," Murray said.

Beth had never seen a double-decker bridge

before. It spanned the river in two layers. There was a train track above a walkway. It looked almost three football fields long. A pair of giant pillars stood on each side of the river. They held up a web of thick cables that suspended the bridge.

"Is Canada on the other side?" Sally asked.

"Yes," said Murray. "Now, I've seen slaves caught here. Some were almost halfway across the bridge. They were pulled back to New York by the slave catchers. But that won't happen to you—not if you take the train."

"But Sally doesn't have a ticket," Beth said.

Murray checked his apron pocket. He pulled his hand out and showed that it was empty. "I left the kitchen in a hurry," he said. "I don't have any money with me."

Beth opened the carriage door and climbed out. "Sally can walk on the bridge," she said. "Can't she?"

"Of course," Murray said. "I'm sure she'll be across in no time."

Sally got out of the carriage next. She adjusted the hood on her blue cloak. "Thank you," Sally said to Murray. "You're a great Underground Railroad conductor. I'm sorry you missed the party."

Murray winked at her. "Mr. Lincoln has strong convictions. He will set things in the country right in regard to slavery," he said. "Come back to Buffalo and visit me on that day."

Patrick waved from inside the carriage. "Goodbye," Patrick said. "God be with—"

Bang! A gunshot split the air. It echoed off the cliffs surrounding them. Beth couldn't tell where the noise had come from.

The carriage horses started to stomp. One of them whinnied.

Murray grabbed the nearest horse's harness. "Whoa, boy," he said.

A man on horseback crested a nearby hill. He wore a large tan hat. His revolver was raised in one hand. In the other he held a whip.

"Sally is going back to her master," the man shouted. "Don't try to stop me, or someone is going to get hurt!"

Beth recognized the voice of Holman Jones.

So did Sally. She seemed to freeze with fear.

The slave catcher draped his whip across the saddle. Then he dug his heels into the horse's side. The horse ran even faster.

Beth started running. She caught Sally's hand and dragged her toward the bridge. "Run," Beth said. "Run!"

Patrick didn't know how to help. He stood in the carriage and watched the horse and rider. Dust and rocks flew up as the horse's hooves pounded the earth. Jones held the gun in the air and waved it.

Murray charged toward him. He shouted, "You rotten excuse for a man!"

As the horse came close, Murray leaped at Jones.

Bang! Another shot went off.

Patrick looked at Murray to see if he'd been shot. But Murray didn't falter. He had hold of Jones's thigh and pulled him off the horse.

The animal bolted past Patrick. He noticed that Jones's whip was hanging off the side of the saddle. The horse ran away into the trees.

The men wrestled and rolled in the mud. Murray got hold of the revolver. He stood and aimed the barrel at Jones. Then Murray began slowly backing away from his enemy.

Patrick noticed Murray was favoring his left leg. He must have been hurt in the scuffle.

The slave catcher lay on his side, breathing heavily. "Don't shoot me!" he cried out.

Murray backed to the cliff's edge. He raised his arm and hurled the weapon into the rushing river below.

In those seconds, Jones leaped to his feet and began running.

"Jones is headed toward the bridge!" Patrick shouted to Murray. "Stop him!"

But Murray wasn't fast enough. His face grimaced in pain with each step he took.

The slave catcher sprinted on.

Patrick climbed into the driver's seat of the carriage. He picked up the reins and snapped them. The horses didn't move.

Please help us, God, Patrick prayed. *Keep Sally safe.*

"Yah!" he shouted. "Giddyap!" He snapped the reins harder. The animals remained still.

Murray's tall form suddenly pushed

him aside. "Hang on!" Murray shouted. He grabbed the reins from Patrick's hands. Murray gave the straps a single flick; the horses moved.

"Hiyah!" Murray shouted.

The horses pulled the carriage close to the bridge entrance. But Jones was still ahead.

Patrick saw a lone figure in a blue cloak entering the walkway. The person dodged quickly between other walkers.

"Look, Murray," Patrick shouted. "It's Sally!"

Suddenly Jones's form appeared on the walkway too. He was only about four people away from Sally.

Murray said, "Go, Patrick. I can't get there in time."

Patrick leaped off the driver's seat. He sprinted toward the walkway.

Jones was moving too fast. Patrick wouldn't be able to stop him.

"There's a slave catcher!" Patrick shouted to the passersby. "Stop him!"

"Where?" a stranger asked. Patrick heard other people ask too. Patrick shouted, "He's wearing the long coat! Wide tan hat!"

The phrase *slave catcher* was suddenly on everyone's lips like wildfire.

An older man in overalls grabbed Jones by the arm. Jones yanked his arm free. The man tried a second time. But the slave catcher twisted away again.

Patrick felt fear grip him. He could not believe what he was seeing.

Jones had Sally—and she wasn't yet

halfway across the bridge. She was still on the New York side.

Jones grabbed both of her shoulders and spun her around. Sally's head was bent low. The hood of the cloak veiled her face.

"I've got you now, Sally Culver!" he shouted. His voice was full of victory.

Sally tilted her head backward so the hood fell off.

Patrick saw a familiar face. He heard a familiar laugh.

Patrick shouted, "Beth!"

Just then a train whistle blew. A rush of steam made a swooshing sound.

Patrick looked up. He saw the train track suspended by thick cables and beams. And a steam engine pulling six passenger cars chugged toward Canada.

A Surprise

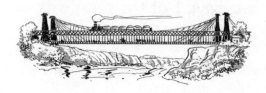

Beth took her eyes off of Holman Jones's face and glanced upward.

Beth felt joy bolster her courage. She offered a silent prayer thanking God for Sally's safety.

"What have you done?" Jones asked. His grip on Beth's shoulders tightened.

Beth winced but didn't cower. "Sally is on that train to freedom," she said. "Let me go."

"I'll take you to South Carolina and sell *you*," Jones said. "I'm not leaving without a slave to sell."

Beth reached out and grabbed the star-shaped badge. She pulled and tore it off the coat. Beth took a deep breath and shouted, "Help! Kidnapper!"

Patrick jumped on Jones's back and tried to cover his eyes. But the man was too strong. He dragged Beth toward the walkway railing. Jones slammed Patrick against it.

Beth heard Patrick's groan and saw her cousin let go.

"Kidnapper!" Patrick shouted. "He's trying to kidnap a free girl!"

This time the people on the walkway became bolder. They quickly surrounded Jones and Beth.

One short, stocky man pushed forward and challenged Jones. He clenched a fist and raised it to Jones's face. He said, "Lincoln gave a speech last night. He told us to stand up for our convictions."

"Then stand up for me, please!" Beth cried.

Murmurs went through the crowd. Beth heard "Yes" and "He's right" and "We've got to help her." People pulled out little American flags and began to wave them.

"We want a bright future," a woman said. "New York doesn't want slavery or kid-nappers."

"Here, here," another person cried.

The stocky man wrestled Jones's left arm. Beth felt Jones's grip loosen. She pulled away. Then two more men strong-armed Jones. They began leading him off the bridge.

Jones protested with curses. He shouted, "I have a legal right to capture slaves!" But the men didn't let him go.

Beth watched as they dragged him off the bridge.

Patrick quickly hugged Beth. "You were brave to swap places with Sally," he said.

"You were brave to try and stop Jones," she said.

Murray slowly limped toward them. Beth hugged the Underground Railroad conductor. She put the Runaway Slave Patrol star badge in his hand. "Throw it into the river," Beth said. "Even though it's legal to capture slaves now, it's wrong."

Murray looked at the badge.

Beth thought she saw a tear slide down his cheek.

Murray dropped the badge over the railing. He brushed his hands together as if to show the job was finished.

"Do you two need a ride back to Buffalo?" Murray asked.

Beth saw the glow of the Imagination Station ahead of them. She heard its familiar hum.

"I think we'll stay here for now," she said. "Thank you."

Patrick shook hands with Murray. "Knocking Jones off the horse was awesome," he said.

"Today our convictions called on us to be courageous," Murray said. "Jones didn't have that kind of power. He was only seeking money. Today freedom won."

Murray said goodbye and limped toward the carriage.

Patrick scratched his head. He seemed to be confused. "Before we get in the Imagination Station," he said, "tell me how you got a train ticket for Sally."

Beth smiled. "Mrs. Lincoln is a lot like Mr. Whittaker," she said. "I put on Sally's blue cape. By habit I checked the pockets."

"She left Sally money?" Patrick said.

Beth nodded. "And she also put in a letter of introduction," Beth said. "Sally will need it to find a job."

Patrick whistled. "A letter from the First Lady of the United States!" he said.

"Ahem," a voice said from behind the cousins. "The precise title would be *future* First Lady. Mr. Lincoln has yet to be inaugurated."

Beth turned toward the voice. Her mouth fell open in wonder. "Eugene?" she said. "You look like a teenager! You should be at least thirty years old."

Beth guessed he had arrived in the Imagination Station.

Eugene was an adult friend of the cousins from Odyssey. He had been with them on their last three adventures.

Patrick said, "What happened?"

"The appropriate question is 'What *didn't* happen?'" Eugene said. "I calculated that I would be my proper age in this adventure. But it appears I was mistaken."

A Surprise

"What are you going to do?" Patrick asked.

"Nothing at the moment," Eugene said. "There's something much more important at stake." He paused and took a long breath. "There's a plot afoot to murder Mr. Lincoln. And we have to stop it!"

To find out more about the next book, *Terror in the Tunnel*, visit TheImaginationStation.com.

Secret Word Puzzle

Beth, Patrick, and Sally traveled north on the Lincoln Special. Just as Sally had to be kept hidden, a secret word is hidden in the following puzzle grid.

Find these words from the story in the puzzle and cross them out:

Niagara   Falls   Beth   Patrick   Sally
Buffalo   Train   Lincoln   Special   Mary
Ticket   Hat   Free

Secret Word Puzzle

F S A L L Y R E

E L P B I R N B

D L A E N A I U

N A T T C M A F

I F R H O I G F

A R I A L O A A

R E C T N M R L

T E K C I T A O

Find the seven letters that are not crossed out. Write them in order in the empty boxes. Then you'll know the secret word.

Answer:

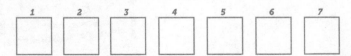

Go to *TheImaginationStation.com*.
Find the cover of this book.
Click on "Secret Word."
Type in the answer,
and you'll receive a prize.